The KNOW-IT-ALLS Go to Sea

BY PETER LIPPMAN

Doubleday & Company, Inc. Garden City, New York

W9-BVH-889

For Millburns
R. + F. + C. + P.N.Ks.

Library of Congress Catalog Card Number 81-43430
Library of Congress Cataloging in Publication Data
Lippman, Peter J.   The Know-It-Alls go to sea.
   Summary: A family of alligators experience misadventures when they take their uncle's boat for a sail.
   [1. Alligators—Fiction. 2. Boats and boating—Fiction] I. Title.   PZ7.L666Ko   [E]   81-43430
ISBN: 0-385-17396-2   Copyright © 1982 by Peter Lippman
All Rights Reserved   Printed in the United States of America   First Edition

The Know-It-Alls, dressed in sailor suits, went to have tea with their uncle, Commander Know-It-All, aboard his boat.

The Commander instructed them to take care of things while he went ashore to buy some supplies.

The family decided to take a quick sail before the Commander returned.

Annie shoveled coal and started up the engine.

Father and Mother Know-It-All steered.

Ernest was the navigator.

"Full steam straight ahead!" shouted Ernest, and the others cheered.

The boat lurched, and there was a big splash. It seemed no one had untied the boat from the dock. "Oh well," said the Know-It-Alls with a shrug. "This town needed a new dock, anyway."

Ernest called down from the crow's nest,
"Closed drawbridge ahead!"
"No matter," said Father Know-It-All. "We'll fit
under it exactly."

Crash! Crunch! Thump! Down came Ernest, and off went the smokestack into the sea. "A short smokestack looks nicer," said Mother.

Soon they found themselves
in the middle of a sailboat race, and they pulled in
front of the lead sailboat to ask directions. The lead
sailboat tried to dodge out of the way while the
others continued on and crossed the finish line.

Next they cruised over to get a better look at a big fish a fisherman had hooked. Unfortunately, they cut the line. "Nothing lost! There are plenty of fish in the sea, I always say," declared Mother Know-It-All.

"Right," agreed Father.

A heavy fog rolled in.

The Know-It-Alls heard a foghorn and saw a searchlight.

"Maybe over there they'll be more helpful with directions than those sore losers in the sailboat," said Mother, as they headed straight for the lighthouse.

Just before they reached it, there was a great *scrunch!* They were stuck fast on a rock. Ernest turned on the ship's radio for entertainment, but he couldn't find any music.

"Storm warning—all boats return to harbor," said the man on the radio.

"Just the same old news I've heard all day," Ernest said.

As rain poured down, the boat began to fill with water. Annie took care of that by drilling some holes in the bottom to let it out.

Lightning flashed. Thunder crashed.
Winds howled and bits of the boat
began to break off. Mother Know-It-All
was getting worried.

"The Commander will wonder
where we are!" she said.
Fortunately, a huge tidal wave
came along and swept the boat up.

They shot past the lighthouse, over the bridge, through the harbor . . .

and landed upside-down on the beach.

At that moment the Commander came puffing up the beach. "This shore duty sure is hard for an old salt like me," he complained. "But I'm glad to see you folks are ready to paint the bottom of the boat."